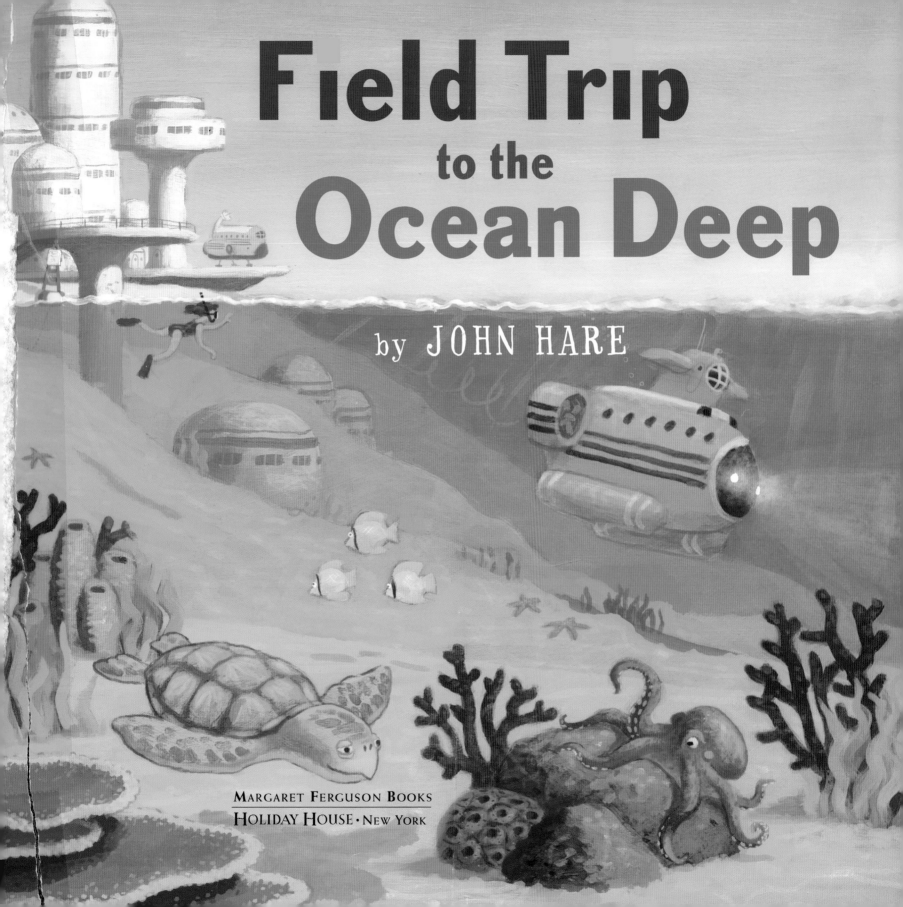

Field Trip
to the
Ocean Deep

by JOHN HARE

MARGARET FERGUSON BOOKS

HOLIDAY HOUSE · NEW YORK

SUBMERSIBLE

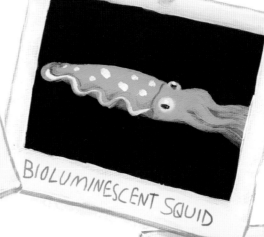
BIOLUMINESCENT SQUID

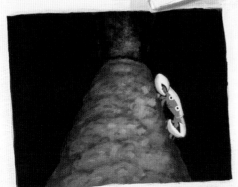
BLACK SMOKER AND CRAB

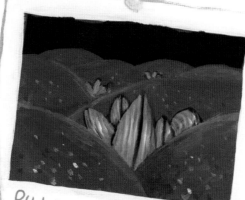
PILLOW LAVA AND CLAMS

GIANT ISOPODS

PLIOSAUR?

ME

ATLANTIS?

For Dad

Margaret Ferguson Books
Copyright © 2020 by John Hare
All Rights Reserved
HOLIDAY HOUSE is registered in the U.S. Patent and Trademark Office.
Printed and bound in July 2020 at Toppan Leefung, DongGuan City, China.
The artwork was created with acrylic paint.
www.holidayhouse.com
First Edition
1 3 5 7 9 10 8 6 4 2

Library of Congress Cataloging-in-Publication Data
Names: Hare, John, (Children's book illustrator), author, illustrator.
Title: Field trip to the ocean deep / by John Hare.
Description: First edition. | New York : Holiday House, [2020] | "Margaret
Ferguson Books." | Audience: Ages 4–8 | Audience: Grades K–1 | Summary:
In this wordless picture book, a student is accidentally left behind on a
field trip to the ocean deep.
Identifiers: LCCN 2019035852 | ISBN 9780823446308 (hardcover)
Subjects: CYAC: School field trips—Fiction. | Ocean—Fiction. | Stories
without words.
Classification: LCC PZ7.1.H3675 Fie 2019 | DDC [E]—dc23
LC record available at https://lccn.loc.gov/2019035852

ISBN: 978-0-8234-4630-8 (hardcover)

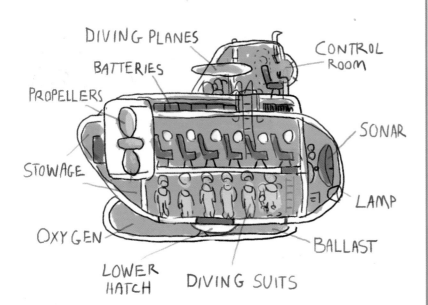

5-UB DEEP SEA BUS

DIVING PLANES
BATTERIES
CONTROL ROOM
PROPELLERS
SONAR
STOWAGE
LAMP
OXYGEN
BALLAST
LOWER HATCH
DIVING SUITS

DS-7 DEEP SEA DIVING SUIT
(YOUTH SIZE)

LAMP/BEACON
OXYGEN
DEEP SEA CAMERA
BATTERY
PRESSURE RESISTANT SHELL
WEIGHTED BOOTS